First Printing, 2013
ISBN 9780615842271

Fingerprint Stories

www.fingerprintstory.com

The Caterpillar Princess

By Hannah &
Dominic **Tuttle**

Fingerprint Stories
www.fingerprintstory.com

It was a sunny day in the town of St. Lunaire and the villagers had all gathered to hear the King of the land speak.

There was laughter and singing and a grand feast for all who attended. Even the King's son, the Great Prince, had joined in the fun. He shared his most courageous stories, much to the delight of all.

Except...

The young Caterpillar Princess was very jealous of all the other villagers who could fly, especially her brother. She would give anything to go on an adventure like he did.

Later that night the King and Prince set about planning their next quest. While the Prince looked over the map, the King pulled aside his most trusted advisor: "My dear Owl, while I'm away, I want you to keep a close eye on my daughter. She is very precious to me and it is for her own safety that she must not leave the castle."

"I will be setting off in a few hours. If there is ANY trouble please let me know immedietly. Owl, I trust you."

After the Princess had calmed down, she stood by her window and began to talk to Owl. The Princess did not like many people, but she didn't mind Owl. Not that she would ever tell him.

The Princess decided to share her plan: "Owl, tomorrow morning I am leaving the castle and not coming back! I am fed up of everyone with wings being free but me. It's not fair!"

The Princess was delighted with her adventure so far. "Isn't this exciting?" She asked the Owl. "My own real quest, and nothing dangerous or even scary ... will you STOP flapping about OWL?! It's fine! I'm strong enough to fight any battle on my own."

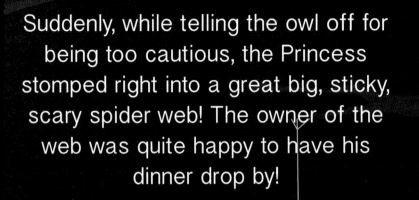

Suddenly, while telling the owl off for being too cautious, the Princess stomped right into a great big, sticky, scary spider web! The owner of the web was quite happy to have his dinner drop by!

The Princess struggled to free herself, but soon found she was not strong enough to break free. "Owl!! Go get help ... please."

As Owl winged away as fast as he could, the Princess sobbed "I wish I had never left home."

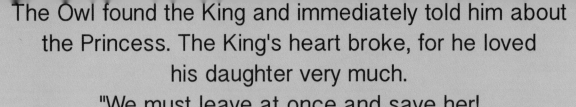

The Owl found the King and immediately told him about
the Princess. The King's heart broke, for he loved
his daughter very much.
"We must leave at once and save her!
But with my back, I fear I will not get there in time."
So the King had an idea...

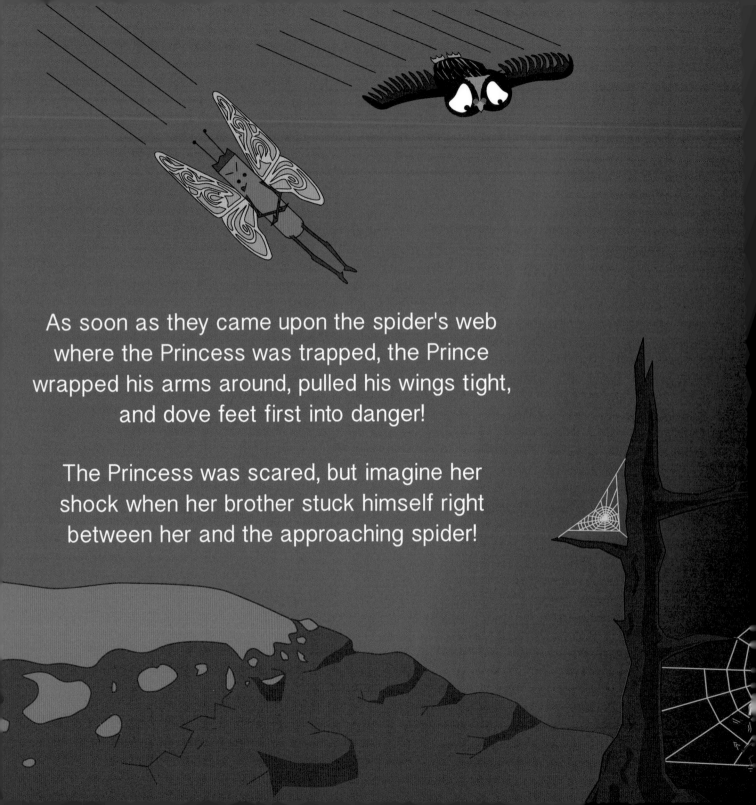

As soon as they came upon the spider's web
where the Princess was trapped, the Prince
wrapped his arms around, pulled his wings tight,
and dove feet first into danger!

The Princess was scared, but imagine her
shock when her brother stuck himself right
between her and the approaching spider!

The Prince yelled,
"Get ready to run!"
Then with all of his strength,
he snapped opened his wings,
tearing the web apart!

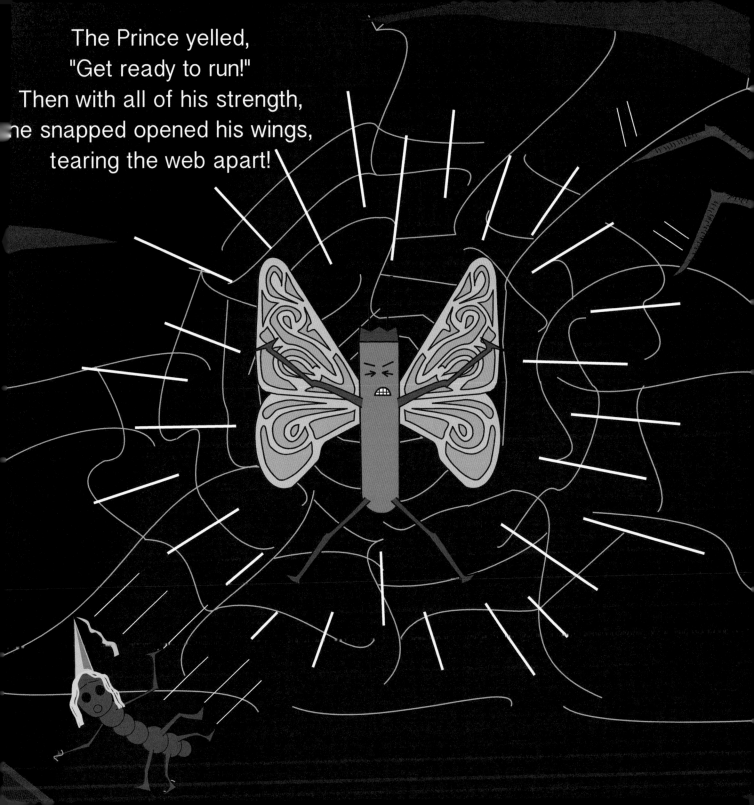

As they made their way back to the castle, the Princess said something quite out of character. "Thank you, Brother ... I'm sorry I ran away. I just wanted to be like you." The Prince replied, "I know it's hard being stuck in the castle. We all had to wait for our wings to grow, too." The Princess looked at him in shock. "You mean, one day, I will have wings?!"

The Prince chuckled, "Of course you'll have wings! You'll be a butterfly just like me! You see, before you can be a butterfly, you have to go through a transformation. It's uncomfortable and boring being in one place and you feel like nothing is happening. But everything is happening. You grow and learn until you're ready to fly! Remember, everyday you're moving forward; everyday has it's own purpose. I know it seems like Father was being hard on you, but he is keeping you safe, just like he kept me safe. A 'thank you' once in a while wouldn't hurt."

The Princess began cheerfully skipping at this news. She vowed to make the best of every day.

That night, the Princess returned to her room and immediately said sorry to her maid for the way she had behaved. They hugged and laughed over a cup of cocoa.

As the Princess was snuggled down in bed, just drifting off to sleep, she felt different: warm and tingly. She slipped into the best dream, full of rainbows and light.

She tossed and turned, unaware of the changes she slept through.

Unaware, that is, until she awoke in the morning to find ...

She was a beautiful BUTTERFLY!

The Princess spent the next day on an exciting new adventure with the King and the Prince!
She felt free and everyday thanked her father for the love and care he continued to show her.

We can learn:

-To be sorry for the times we have been impatient and rude to others, like the Caterpillar Princess.

-To thank our friends and family who take care of us, even when it seems like we're trapped.

-To be patient as we learn and grow, trusting that we will someday be ready to do what we have been made to do!